# Maisy Goes to London

## Lucy Cousins

### WALKER BOOKS
AND SUBSIDIARIES

LONDON • BOSTON • SYDNEY • AUCKLAND

This Walker book belongs to:

...................................................................................

First published 2016 by Walker Books Ltd
87 Vauxhall Walk, London SE11 5HJ

This edition published 2017

2 4 6 8 10 9 7 5 3 1

© 1990 – 2017 Lucy Cousins

This book has been typeset in Gill Sans MT Schoolbook and Lucy Cousins font.
Lucy Cousins font © 1990 – 2017 Lucy Cousins
Handlettering by Lucy Cousins.

Maisy ™. Maisy is a trademark of Walker Books Ltd, London.

The right of Lucy Cousins to be identified as author/illustrator of this
work has been asserted by her in accordance with the
Copyright, Designs and Patents Act 1988.

London Bus Stop logo ® Transport for London

Printed in China

British Library Cataloguing in Publication Data:
a catalogue record for this book is available from the British Library.

ISBN 978-1-4063-7220-5

www.walker.co.uk

How exciting! The city is **So** noisy!
"Let's take the bus," says Maisy.

vrooooom!

toot, toot!

brrmmm, brmm!

First stop, Piccadilly Circus.

# Look at all the flashing lights!

Next they walk to Trafalgar Square to see Nelson's Column. It's very tall!

"I love this big, friendly lion", says Charley. Maisy snaps a photo.

click!

Then they go inside to look at all the paintings in the National Gallery.

There are so many amazing pictures.
Maisy likes the **sunflowers** best.

After a picnic lunch,
    they play in the park...

and Tallulah
feeds the ducks.

buzz, buzz!

quack, quack!

Wow! It's Buckingham Palace,
where the Queen lives.
Hello, Your Majesty.

The palace guard is very serious.
He doesn't even smile.

Maisy takes another photo.

Next, they walk along the River Thames and see the Houses of Parliament.

Maisy and her friends go on a river boat.

Look, the gates are opening on Tower Bridge!

At the Tower of London,
Maisy takes some photos
of the ravens.

click!

Cyril and Charley
love the Beefeater's
colourful uniform.

Next,
they go
down, down, down
to the underground.

It's very crowded on the
tube train.
"Hold on tight!" says Maisy.

On the riverbank,
they buy some snacks. Yum!

"Let's go to the aquarium,"
says Tallulah.

ting,
ting!

Amazing! What a lot of fish!
"The shark's teeth look very sharp!" says Cyril.
Soon it's time to go,
but first they visit the gift shop.

Before they go home,
Maisy and her friends get one
last photo on the bridge.

What a brilliant day!
"I LOVE London," says Maisy.

Piccadilly Circus

Nelson's Column

Tower Bridge

Hello, raven!

Big Ben

Buckingham Palace

At the aquarium

We love London!

I ♥ London

# Lucy Cousins

is the multi-award-winning creator of much-loved character Maisy. She has written and illustrated over 100 books and has sold over 30 million copies worldwide.

## Other books by Lucy Cousins:

978-1-4063-2783-0

978-1-4063-5802-5

978-1-4063-3965-9

978-1-4063-6429-3

978-1-4063-6553-5

978-1-4063-7152-9

Available from all good booksellers